I cried... But I
NEVER
"GAVE UP"

A Novel by
D M Cummings

D M Cummings

Also by D M Cummings

Fiction

Is Real Love Worth My Life?

Diamond's Pearl

Take a Walk in my Shoes

An imprint of The World Is Mine (TWIM) Publishing
PO Box 3086
Akron, OH 44309

For information about special discounts for bulk purchases please contact The World is Mine Publishing at dmcummingstwim@gmail.com.

Book cover design by A.P. Bolden

Manufactured in the United States of America

Library of Congress Cataloging-in-publication Data has been applied for.

Chapter 1 -A Teenage Love

Mary grew up in a household with both of her parents who were supportive of all her necessary wants and needs and she sometimes took advantage of situations. They couldn't live as they wanted, as Mary's mother was a teen mom and was on Government assistance for some time, but she was fortunate to marry her daughter's father. Mary was very sneaky, talked back a lot and her dad spoiled her since she was his "baby girl." He thought that she could do nothing wrong. She was rarely in trouble, even when she did things she should have been punished for.

Mary always enjoyed going to football and basketball games with her friends, and her parents had no problem with that. One day Mary and her girls went to a football game, just hanging around the concession stand, not buying, just observing. There was this one guy who came to all the games that caught her attention. He was brown skinned, stood about five feet and eleven inches tall, and from his muscular arms and legs, it was obvious that he spent time in the gym. He had to be in high school because she had never seen him during her school day and junior high students were not permitted to venture to the high school side, so that would make sense. She had asked her girls, and no one knew who he was. This particular day, Mary had some courage and decided to speak to him. He smiled and he was finer than she had thought the first couple of glances that she had of him. She started making small talk, asking him which school he attended, and she was correct, he attended Roosevelt, just as she did. He was in the tenth grade, and everyone called him Swav. She didn't tell him that she had just turned fourteen three weeks prior and in the eighth grade, not just yet. She didn't look her age at all. She stood five feet and four inches tall; she kept her hair in braids, half up and half down. It was summer, so she had on a crop top shirt, a pair of jogging shorts that showed off her curves and a pair of black and white, high-top Dunks. Swav gave her a good look up and down and asked her age, because her physique was nice, but her conversation and all the giggling came across as a little immature. Mary told him that she was fifteen and a half. His boys came over and interrupted their conversation. "Come on Swav, we had to come and see what was taking you so long to get some nachos and cheese." They laughed.

"I'm good man, I got caught up in a conversation." He turned his attention back to Mary "alright shorty, I'll see you around." Mary frowned in confusion; she just knew that he wasn't going to just brush her off like that. Her girls laughed. "Girl, I guess he wasn't interested, or he knew you were lying about your age. "I'm not worried, I saw him looking." Mary confidently replied.

The next few games, Mary made sure that she was extra cute, and she also made sure that she spoke to Swav. He was always with his boys, he was cordial, but kept it moving. She was ready to give up, but one day she was headed from the bathroom and Swav was coming towards her alone. "Oh, you don't have your bodyguards with you today, huh?" Mary asked jokingly. Swav laughed, "Yeah, not today." "So, can I get a few minutes of your time?" Mary asked seductively, while running her fingers through her braids. "I was getting ready to run to the bathroom real quick." "Well, why don't you give me your number and we can talk later?" To her surprise, he was willing to give her the number. "I can do that." Mary pulled out her phone, unlocked it and handed it to Swav so that he could add his number. She didn't tell her girls just yet, because she wanted to make sure that he had given her the correct number and to see if the conversation would go anywhere. She didn't want to come off as being "thirsty", so she waited until the next day to call. The conversation went well, and they started calling each other almost every day. Within two months, she considered him her boyfriend. Swav would still act differently around his boys when she was around, but he had told her that he didn't like his boys in his relationship business because they were on a different side of the tracks. She didn't ask what that meant, she just rolled with it. They were really into each other but they both had many secrets and their relationship started off with lies. He told her that he was in a work study program which only kept him in school a few hours per day, but, in reality, he didn't go to school on a regular basis; therefore, he would never see her in school. She knew that she wasn't allowed on the high school side; therefore, she would never see him either, which meant his lie worked in both of their favors.

After about seven months of dating Mary found out the truth about Swav and the reason why he rarely came to school. He was hanging in the streets with his boys all day, doing things that he had no business doing. Mary was cool with his choices because although her parents gave her everything that she wanted, Swav was giving her even more and he kept plenty of money in her pockets for whatever she wanted. When she started high school, she was the finest. She always kept her hair, nails and toes done making sure that everyone knew that Swav was her man. By her tenth-grade year, Mary was pregnant and surprisingly, she was as happy as can be. Swav was a little concerned because he wasn't trying to mess up her life. He wanted her to graduate and make sure she would be able to get a decent job to take care of herself. "When is the baby due?" Swav asked.

"June seventh". Mary replied with a smile.

"YES!!" Swav tilted his head back and closed his eyes, while pumping his fist in the air. "That way you'll graduate before you have the baby." Mary became silent for a few seconds, shaking her head as the smile faded from her face.

"Well... about that." Mary sighed. "I lied to you when we first met." She put her hand over her forehead remembering that she never told him her real age. "I'm only sixteen, but I will be turning seventeen in April."

"Maaan, whaat?! You tryna set me up to go to jail? I'm about to be nineteen years old!"

"I for real, for real forgot I told you that when we met. I just knew you were older and probably wouldn't have given me the time of day, if you knew my real age."

"Dudes get locked up for mess like this and this ain't what I do. And you are right, I would <u>not</u> have given you the time of day. I'mma holla at you later, I gotta get my head right." Clearly with a disappointed look on his face, Swav left to meet his boys.

> *People need to be honest with each other, if it's meant to be, it will be. When you lie, you don't always remember what you said and small lies can lead to something big, and someone could get hurt or in serious trouble.*

Chapter 2- Where it all began

Mary, almost seventeen years old was having a few complications with her pregnancy, but was determined to keep her baby, to keep Swav. She didn't work and it was the spring before her junior year, and she was placed on bed rest for the last two months of her pregnancy. She used this to her advantage. Swav waited on her hand and foot to make sure she and their baby were safe and healthy. Her parents tried to be supportive and help as much as they could, but Mary thought that she was grown, and wanted to make her own decisions, although she was still a child. She didn't like her parent's rules, and she didn't want to hear anything they had to say about her high school sweetheart and the father of her unborn child. Mary had a rough delivery, but Swav was there by her side every moment. She gave birth to a seven pound and three ounces little boy, who she named Damion. Mary was able to graduate from high school with the help of her parents and Swav who took turns keeping her son. Swav loved his son and made sure that he and his woman didn't want or need anything. When Damion was five, his father that he loved and wanted to be by his side every moment, went to prison at the age of twenty-three and was sentenced to twelve years for the bad decisions that he made. Instead of Mary using the ten thousand dollars that Swav had saved and stashed away for an emergency such as this, to get him an attorney, she let him get a state appointed attorney. Since he didn't get the representation that he needed, he felt that he was given too much time for the crime that he had committed. Mary was selfish and too focused on herself and materialistic things to be concerned about what was best for Swav. She was left to raise her son on her own and couldn't afford her current living arrangements. Although her parents willingly opened their doors for their daughter and grandson, she now refused their help because of the various negative comments that they continuously made about Swav. Mary applied for government assistance, which would allow her to continue to live independently and not have to hear what her parents had to say.

Young Damion was a splitting image of Swav, and Mary resented her son for it, and at times it showed. Her parents would babysit a lot at the beginning, which allowed her to hang out in the clubs partying, blowing money, with no income to replace it. They felt sorry for her and didn't want their grandson being left with just anyone or being left home alone, something she had done in the past. Mary was making bad decisions because she was messed up mentally and moving off hurt as she thought Swav would be there forever. She was very angry with Swav for leaving them, but this is who she chose. He made sure that he reminded her that things could have been different if she had paid for the representation instead of allowing the public defender to represent him. She was being selfish and now paying the price of being alone. She knew the risky lifestyle that he was living, but she thought it was cute. They had a nice apartment; Damion had the best shoes and clothes that money could buy. He even had a little gold chain with his name on it. Swav bought Mary new clothes, shoes, and stylish handbags regularly, but it all ended just as fast as it started. After Swav's arrest, she would still go to the clubs with all her fancy jewelry, nice clothes, shoes, and purses like nothing had changed, enjoying every ounce of the attention that she received from the men and even the eye rolls from some women. Mary would often come in late, with men so disrespectfully, even on nights that Damion was home. He would hide his head under the cover with the pillows over his ears to drown out the noises that were too mature for his young ears. Mary's parents thought that if she kept her own son more often, maybe she'd gain more respect for herself, her body and her child and would stop, but she didn't. As Damion aged and matured, he lost a lot of respect for his mother. Brian, who everyone called B, the last guy Mary brought home, never left her governed subsidized home. Mary spent a lot of time in her bedroom with the door shut while B was around, leaving Damion to fend for himself. He would eat peanut butter and crackers when there was peanut butter or butter and jelly sandwiches when they were out of peanut butter. Since Mary wasn't always working, she would sell some of her food stamps to help with her income-based rent, gas money and discounted utilities. This never left enough stamps for food for the month. By the age of twenty-one Mary was pregnant once again, but this time, by B. She gave birth to Damion's sister, Neisha, two months after she turned twenty-two. B stayed around and was in fact, a good father to them both, but he had a lot of flaws. B never finished high school, only had a ninth-grade education, and never had the desire to work a nine to five. He loved living in the streets. Prior to Mary meeting B, she and Damion were struggling so much that some days his only meals came from school. Damion had to wear tight, high-water jeans that he tried to droop to make them seem long enough since that was the style, but the kids could tell the difference and he was teased. The kids would say corny things like "hey Damion man, Noah's ark already came, it's not going to be another flood." Since named brand shoes weren't in the budget, his mother refused to buy them. He tried to wear his dad's old shoes that he found stored in an old tote in the basement, but they were still a little too big. He begged his grandmother to get him the new cool black and white light up Sketchers, but to all the kids who wore the Jordan's and Air Forces laughed at him and thought they were lame, even though they cost just as much and were advertised by Snoop Dogg. They would tease him and even had a little song they would sing "head, shoulders, knees and toes, what are those- twinkle toes?" while pointing at his shoes and laughing hysterically. Damion hated his life and started acting out so that he would be sent home or even suspended.

As Damion matured, around eleven and a half years old, B thought he would try to teach him the game of the streets, but

Damion heard stories about the
misfortunes of a lot of the young boys in
the neighborhood who had passed away.
He knew why his father was locked up, and
he wasn't interested. B once took Damion
to the store with him and asked him to do
something that he was totally against. "So,
are you ready to become a man?" B asked.
"Nope, I'm still a kid." Damion responded as
they looked eye to eye and Damion keeping
a straight face as he shook his head from
side to side. B laughed.
"You see that guy over there with the gray
shirt." Damion looked and responded,
yeah..." B handed him a bag.
"Go over there and give him this and tell
him it's from B and whatever he gives you is
yours. It's that easy. Go ahead." B says.
"Does my mom know that you want me to
do stuff like this?"
"Yeah, your mom wants you to be a man."
"I'm pretty sure she doesn't." Damion
jumped out of the car and headed home. B

sat in the car in disbelief. *I can't believe that ungrateful little….* He shook his head. He took care of his own business and went home to have a talk with Mary about her son. Damion wanted his own money and nicer clothes, so he didn't have to depend on B buying for him on the regular, but he didn't want to take that chance.

        Damion made it home first and was really upset when he came into the house.
"Mom, can we talk?"
"Boy, about what?" she asked with her hands on her hips.
"Your boyfriend."
"Who, your dad?"
"B ain't none of my dad. My dad loves me and would never try to make me do no foul mess that he just asked me to do."
"If your dad loved you, then he would be here" she said while rolling her eyes, "but anyways, what are you talking about?"
Damion closed his eyes to hold back the

tears and squeezed his lips tight so he
wouldn't disrespect his mother. "He tried to
get me to sell drugs."
"Boy please! He loves you, and you need to
stop acting like he don't do nothing for this
family. B wouldn't ask you to do anything
like that."
"Well, he did and that's why I walked
home." Mary crossed her arms over her
chest and smacked her lips. "Who do you
think keeps the lights and heat on around
here? Just go to your room," Mary said to
Damion in disgust.
"Oh, that's all you care about, huh?"
Damion gave her a confused look, smacked
his lips, shook his head, and walked to his
room slamming the door. His grandparents
made him go to church every Sunday that
he spent with them and had always talked
to him about doing the right thing and not
feeling pressured by anyone. They made
him understand that he would be the one
to have to pay for the consequences and

choices that he made. His father had also made it clear to his son that he'd made some bad choices which caused him to be where he is and what he expected out of his son which was for him to go to school, get a legit job, graduate high school, go to college, or take up a trade that would help him make a good living. When B finally came in, he sat down at the table with a disgusted look on his face.

"Now, what's wrong with you?" Mary asked.

"Man, you need to do something about your son."

"What you mean?," Mary asked.

"He is soft, and such a mama's boy. He ain't gon' be no real man when he grows up. He running around here acting like he grown, but when the opportunity comes for him to step up, he runs like a little girl."

"What happened?"

"I'm out here trying to take him under my wing and show him how to make some

money and be a man, and he acting like a lil'
girl". Mary sat down on B's lap and put her
arm around his neck.
"Yeah, he told me you asked him...
B cut her off. "See this is what I'm talking
about, he ran right in here crying to his
mama. You need to stop babying that boy
or I'm gon' have to stop helping you with
him."
"Don't be like that. You know that he be
missing his daddy sometimes and my
mom's..." Mary rolled her eyes. "Man, she
be all in his ear trying to make him like
them. He'll come around, just give him
some time."

> *Women need to stop talking down on
> their children's fathers to their kids, if
> you feel some negative type of way
> about them, you should keep your
> thoughts and opinions to yourself.
> The child will see the true person in
> them themselves. Women should also*

stop putting these men before their children. When a child comes to tell you something you need to listen, even if you don't want to deal with it. You should not sweep things under the rug as if they didn't happen. A child should always be seen and heard and should always feel as if they have someone to talk to confidentially, if they have a problem; especially, when an adult is trying to make them do something they know is not right. All money is not good money especially if it can have a negative effect on their lives. Sometimes struggling makes you appreciate what you have even more.

Damion tried his best to avoid B whenever possible, which wasn't usually that hard, considering most of the time he would just be waking up around three-thirty in the afternoon, when Damion came in from school. Damion would go straight to his room to do homework or just to not be bothered with anyone. Usually, around six or seven in the evening, B would leave and wouldn't return until late at night or early the next morning, which was fine with Damion. Most of the time when he came in too late, he'd have to hear the arguing, usually about another woman. Nights that B didn't come home, Damion would listen to his mom as she called B's cell phone over and over expressing her thoughts and feelings out loud about how she hated it when he didn't answer his phone and then she'd pray that everything was alright. He hated seeing his mom like this and vowed that he would never put her or any woman that he dealt with through that. This was something that Mary was choosing to deal with.

> *We may not realize it, but our*
> *children watch everything that we do.*

Some of them learn what not to do and others mimic what they see. We must try to be positive role models for our children and set good examples, if we expect them to grow up to be something. None of us are perfect, and life is a learned lesson, but if you see yourself following the same negative circle you must find a way to go North, if not for you, do it for your children.

Chapter 3 – No support within us

Why is it so hard for black people to support each other? Instead of being proud of each other's accomplishments and success, we hate, rob, or steal and sometimes even kill. Innocent lives are being taken over jealousy and materialistic things. The taker usually ends up in jail and now two people that could have made a positive impact in life are gone. There are no winners in the end.

Damion and his mother lived in the "hood" since he could remember, they didn't have a lot, but they got by. He attended the schools in his neighborhood where the conditions were horrible. There was a metal detector at the door where they entered the building that each student had to walk through, periodically there were police dogs roaming the building with a police escort, random bookbag and locker searches were being done and the graduation rate was not that great. The lunches were horrible, so most days Damion tried to eat a decent breakfast to get him through the day. He had gotten used to the environment because this is what he had become accustomed to, but he wanted to be better. He worked a part time job under the table, at a small Moms and Pops restaurant; although, he wasn't of age, the owner knew B and saw that Damion wasn't trying to live that life and allowed him to come by some evenings to clean up the restaurant for a couple of dollars. The corner boys ridiculed and teased him for working and because he didn't want to hang in the streets with all the guys with their pants hanging off their butts, drinking, smoking, and skipping school. Everyday his walk to school was a task. They would call out things to him like "hey trash boy come over here and hit this blunt, it'll make some hair grow on your chest". He would just reply "I'm cool" and continue his walk to school. They would laugh hysterically and say that he was a "lame" and that he thought he was better than them. Most of the guys that hung out on the corners had dropped out of school, were held back, or didn't have an interest in attending every day and weren't doing anything productive or positive with their lives. Damion started wearing his large headphones, not always listening to music, but making it look as if he were, giving him the opportunity to ignore their ignorant comments. When he just didn't want to hear their immaturity, he'd listen to old raps from Tupac and Biggie to get his mind in a comfortable place. His moto was, as long as they didn't touch him, they could say what they wanted. One day as he was walking to school CJ, one of the corner boys tried to block him from getting passed, Damion rolled his eyes "man what?" he asked.

"What you listening to?" and he tried to take his headphones. Another guy, Lonnie, who also stood on the corner saw potential in Damion and wanted to see one of them get out of the hood, so he intervened.

"Man" smacking his lips "leave lil' dude alone."

"Why you sticking up for that lil trash picker uppin' mama's boy?" asked CJ.

"Man, you a sucka" Lonnie replied as he stood between CJ and Damion putting his arm on Damion's shoulder. "Learn something at school today lil' man. You hear me?" Lonnie wasn't that much bigger than CJ, but apparently, he respected what he said because he didn't say anything else. Damion was ready for whatever as he knew how to handle his own, but he was confused. He hurriedly walked away, glancing back quickly with his music turned off to hear if someone was coming up from behind him. From that day forward every time he walked past the guys on the corner, Lonnie always threw his head up to Damion to say what's up and all the name calling, and harassment stopped. Lonnie was basically hanging on the corner to play the role of being a thug to fit in or to be part of something, but he was actually very intelligent, he just knew how to play the thug role well. Lonnie was once Damion before he moved from Chicago to the neighborhood, and he knew how it felt to be picked on because he was trying to do the right thing and it caused him to make some bad decisions. He'd learned from his mistakes and didn't want to see Damion go down that same road. He had been held back once in high school and eventually dropped out and went to the juvenile detention center for several months but went back to school and received his diploma at the age of twenty.

> *"Sometimes it just takes one person out of the crew to stand up for someone who is being bullied for it to stop. You don't always have to join in when you know it's not right and most of the time you are not the only one feeling that way. Usually, bullies are just trying to get the attention off themselves and the focus on others. Also, if you are working towards something and you get set back or have a goal that you are determined to reach, keep working at it and don't give up!!"*

Chapter 4- Not your child's child

Damion had a few friends that he hung out with every now and then, but sometimes when he wanted to leave the house, his mother made it hard for him. Mary would tell him that he couldn't leave because she wanted to follow B around or go hang out at the clubs, but she had no one to watch Neisha. B didn't want his daughter to spend too much time with Mary's parents because he didn't want them in their business. Damion loved his little sister dearly but hated that he was forced to spend time with her. Some days Mary told him that he had to come right home from school because she had "stuff to do" and he needed to watch his sister. "Mom, I was planning on going over to the restaurant after school to make a couple of dollars because I am trying to save up for a new pair of shoes and then I wanted to go over my friend's house to play video games."

"B is going to buy both of you a new pair of shoes next week. And don't you have something better to do with your time than play some dumb video games? All that can wait, and those twenty dollars a day that he gives you when you go down there to work, is nothing but chump change." She always had an excuse as to why he needed to come home.

"Well, why don't you pay me to watch your child because I don't have any kids." Mary snapped her head back and rolled her eyes.

"You better watch your mouth, or you're going to wish you would've. As much as I do around here, that is the least you can do for us. I cook every day, make sure your clothes are clean and... I don't owe you any explanations, just stay here and watch her and I will see you when I get back." This was beginning to be an every other day thing, especially on the weekend. Damion was getting tired of it. He was trying to make friends and stay away from the house, but his mother was really making it complicated.

Some nights Mary would come in and it was obvious that she had been partying too hard. If Neisha was crying, she wouldn't attempt to comfort her, but would expect Damion to, although he had to get up to go to school the next day. He felt some kind of way about that, but what could he do? He couldn't just let his baby sister cry and not be fed. Neisha slept in his room several nights during the week and really became attached to her brother. Damion spent more time with Neisha than she did with her parents.

We as parents need to stop putting our kids off on their older siblings. If you must go to work and don't have a sitter, or need to run to the store or something quick is fine, but not allowing them to be a child because you want to hang in the streets is not fair. This could cause the child to resent their siblings or harm them.

Chapter 5 Trapped within the system

Mary's life had become a mess and she had no desire to grow. Her parents had tried to talk to her and offered guidance, but she didn't want their help. She was comfortable with her lifestyle. She had been on housing assistance or rented since she was on her own at the age of seventeen. Back in the day, she and Swav had discussed buying a house but, since he was gone, she never had the desire because assistance was readily available. B never mentioned moving her to a better place. He was able to pay all her bills for less than two hundred dollars a month, which made him look good and kept extra money in his pocket. When Mary did work, she worked a lot of factory jobs and when she was laid off or quit, she always had the system to fall back on. She started working as a lunch lady at the neighborhood elementary school because it was convenient. She only worked about four hours a day with no weekends, and she had all the holidays off as well as the summers. Luckily, her government benefits would increase during the summer since she was no longer working. When B was around, he paid her bills, which allowed her to save a little money for a rainy day. This worked out great for her. Mary never really understood the real struggle because she always received government benefits or had a man taking care of her and she had become complacent and had no desire to change or want more. She tried to get better jobs in the past, but when she was turned down because she only had a high school education and a poor work history, she never took it personal. Mary thought that was how society was designed and those jobs just weren't meant for her.

Mary did want the best for her daughter and did everything that she possibly could to ensure that she didn't have to endure any trials or tribulations. Damion's sister Neisha got and did whatever she wanted, and Mary supported whatever it was she wanted to do. She had a child when she was fifteen by a corner boy, and her mother wanted better for her because she saw herself in her daughter and wanted her to have a better life than she did. She enjoyed the extra food stamps and the decrease in her ninety-six dollar a month rent, but she didn't want her to struggle or to rely on a man to survive. Mary helped Neisha with her baby as much as possible and sent her to a private school on a scholarship to ensure that she received a better education. In Mary's eyes, Neisha was going to do the right thing because she had another life to care for. Mary felt that if Neisha got a good education, she and her child would be better off in life, but she was going to enjoy the extra benefits as long as she could. She also knew that if things didn't work out for the best, Neisha could also get approved for housing assistance. Damion, on the other hand was a "man" and he had to learn how to survive.

> *"It's alright to utilize housing assistance, food stamps and other government benefits because that's what they are designed for, but we need to learn to use them as a steppingstone and not as a crutch. Assistance is available to inspire you to do better but we seem to become complacent when life is made easier, and we don't want to grow. We need to work toward owning something so we can leave our children a legacy. We also need to stop acting like our sons aren't as worthy as our daughters. We must give them the*

same opportunities, maybe we would
have more successful black men if
they had more support."

Chapter 6- Real fathers' matter

Damion, who was now fourteen years old, hated going to his mother's house because it wasn't a home. B was still around for the most part, although he didn't say much to Damion as his presence irritated him. Damion started hanging out at the parks after school or just walking around the neighborhood, but he didn't see a lot of positive things going on and didn't want to get in the middle of any mess so that ended quickly. He started going to a friend's house after school to play video games and would sometimes stay the night but there was a lot of traffic, coming and going. On the weekends, boy oh boy... they had parties. Damion felt safer at his mother's house. His friend's parents allowed them to drink and engage in whatever other activities that they wanted to because they were into their own

company, and they didn't really care. It was
fun at first but after a while it became too
much. All the men had weapons on their
hips and the women had the foulest
mouths. This was a super negative
environment that he didn't want to be
around, but it was better than his mother's
house, at the beginning. His grandparents
didn't live that close, but he had learned to
catch the bus as well as how to get a Lyft or
Uber. He would sometimes use those
means of transportation to get to their
home. Damion started spending a lot more
time with his grandparents, helping them
by cutting the grass or other small tasks
around the house to get some extra money.
B tried to keep money in his pocket, but he
didn't want anything from him or nothing to
do with him. Every time Damion would
walk into a room with B and his mother, B
would stare at him as if he was disgusted,
and his mother would start acting funny. He

had gotten in touch with his father, which is what he had been wanting for years. Swav used to call his son every weekend prior to them moving, which at that time he lost contact. Damion reached out to him when he was a little older, about ten or eleven, to let him know that they had moved and their new phone number, but once Mary had gotten really close with B she stopped accepting his calls and eventually let their landline get cut off and Swav didn't have her cell phone number. He had tried writing a few times, but Damion stopped receiving the letters and from the negative things that his mother was saying, he thought that his father had forgotten about him.

Swav went down every avenue that he could think of to find his son, and finally decided to reach out to Damion's grandparents, even though he knew that he wasn't one of their favorites. He was able to find their number on Google and had called a few times. Once he was finally able to speak with Damion's grandmother, he informed her that he was trying to get in touch with Damion. His grandmother told Swav that he was coming over on the weekends, not discussing any of his personal business, but gave him the address so that he could write and let him know that she didn't mind him periodically calling to speak with his son. Damion and his father started writing once a month and the letters would go to his grandparents' home so that his mother or B couldn't intercept the mail or try to read it. Swav would also call every other weekend and Damion told his father everything that was going on before he explained that he had been writing to him for years and asked why he never wrote back. Damion knew it was some shade as to why he stopped hearing from his father, he knew that he would never forget about him. "I stopped receiving letters years ago, around the time my mom had Neisha. Her sucka as..." Damion caught himself. "Her boyfriend probably took them or told her to stop giving them to me because he wanted to be my dad so bad, but I'm just not feeling him, and I wish he would just leave". All Swav could do was listen as he cried silent tears. Damion broke the silence by telling him how he was staying over his friend's and about all the different game systems that he had, how it was fun at first, and all the activities that had taken place. Swav knew the kid's parents whose house he was visiting and advised him to stay away from that environment before he ended up where he was or worse.

Damion had really started to become depressed and speaking to his father was the mental release that he needed. He hadn't cried so hard since his father was arrested. Swav hated himself for not making better decisions and for getting "caught up". He resented Mary even more for not looking out for him or bringing his son to see him after everything he had done for her. He wanted to be there for his son, but he couldn't. He tried reaching out to Mary on the number that Damion had recently given him, to see what was going on in her head, but she wouldn't accept any of his phone calls. He was able to call on a prepaid line and once he started speaking, she would hang up the phone. He made a few calls to a couple of the guys that he had run with when he was in the streets to find out who B was, and how he could get some help for his son. He didn't want him to end up like he did. He wanted something positive for his son, who was visibly trying to do something with his life.

A child's home should be a safe place. If they don't have a place to go and feel safe, they will sometimes look in the wrong place or with the wrong person.

Damion slowly started bringing gym bags of his clothes when he came to visit his grandparents. He started staying with them every weekend, then throughout the summer and finally he convinced them to let him switch schools and attend a school in their district which was in a much better neighborhood. He was much happier than staying with his mother, in his bedroom and not talking to anyone. He and Neisha got along well, but she was such a daddy's girl that he didn't feel as if he could talk to her about everything. She just didn't understand. Damion felt like a loner and was grateful for his grandparents. Mary didn't even look for her son, she was glad that he was gone. Mary's mother eventually called to let her know where Damion was and she just replied with "Oh, ok".

Chapter 7- Back to the basics

Damion's grandfather had started to become ill; he was in and out of the hospital and his grandmother was doing a lot to take care of him. Damion had gotten a job at a hamburger place and would help his grandmother when he could, but she wanted him to focus on his education and to enjoy his childhood. Damion made a few new friends in the neighborhood that he would go to the mall with, or to the arcade to play video games or they would sometimes go skating. These were activities that he didn't get to do when he lived with his mother because there really wasn't anyone in that neighborhood that he took a liking to and there was always some sort of drama whenever people tried to have fun in that neighborhood. He even had a girlfriend that he spent a lot of time with. She was a beautiful high school cheerleader for both football and basketball, which were the sports that he also played. She had a caramel complexion, with jet black, shoulder length hair that she always wore in a ponytail. She wore a pair of the newest style, clear framed eyeglasses and was really into her education. Although her name was Starlet, everyone called her Star. Star was a straight A student and she and Damion always talked about going to college.

That summer Damion's grandfather passed away and his grandmother was really having a hard time dealing with his absence. She had been with her husband since she was sixteen years old. Although, she had Damion to keep her company, it just wasn't the same. Mary had started to come around and trying to reach out to Damion since she and B were having all kinds of issues since Neisha had gotten pregnant and B was constantly going in and out of jail because of his bad choices, which she didn't mind because she knew that Swav would be getting out soon. She wanted to set the image that she was doing a great job as a mother. Mary and Damion were on speaking terms, but he enjoyed staying with his grandmother. During the middle of Damion's eleventh grade school year his grandmother became ill with Covid19, and Damion had to move back home with his mother. He resented this but really didn't have a choice. His father had been released but he was not in a place where Damion could stay with him, and it was about a two-hour drive to where he was staying. When Damion returned to his mother's house he was disappointed to see that his room had been turned into a baby's room. There was cartoon character wallpaper plastered all over the walls, a baby crib and teddy bears' everywhere. "So, where am I supposed to sleep? I'm not staying in here with all this baby stuff," said Damion. Neisha, who was walking around with her belly poked out laughed. "We didn't think that you were ever coming back, sooo... I started making a room for my child." Damion shook his head, "man... you done ruined your life. Who you pregnant by? And what did your daddy have to say about that?" Neisha avoided the first question. "Oh, Brian was pissed when he found out" she said with a smile. "Found out what, that you were pregnant or who you were pregnant by." She laughed, "Both. He used to bring all these young boys over here to hang out, and me and one of them linked up." "How old is young?" "Well... he's seventeen now." "Um... so he's my age." "Don't even trip." "I'm not saying anything. What school does he go to? Do I know him?" "You probably do," she replied nonchalantly.

"Well, what I do know is that if he was over here with B he was up to no good and probably is no good for you, which is probably why he is pissed. He doesn't want his "princess" with no thug." Damion began to laugh.
"What's so funny?"
"It's just funny how the tables turn, he wanted me to be in these streets, but doesn't want his daughter messing with anyone out there. I am so glad that I left when I did. There's no telling how my life would be right now."

Damion finished out his school year at the school by his grandmother's home and would check on her periodically. She made him keep his distance even after she was better because she didn't want to take any chances of getting Damion sick. She also wanted some time alone to grieve for her late husband and to go through his things and reminisce privately. Damion would sometimes stay with his friends that lived closer to his grandmother when he had school the next day because when he stayed at his mom's, he would have to get up extra early to catch the bus, but to him, it was worth the hassle to stay at that school.

The upcoming school year, and Damion's senior year, he enrolled into his original school, the high school closest to his mother's house. He had matured nicely since ninth grade. He was a lot taller, had a nice physique, deep dimples, and the prettiest smile.

Sometimes the environment that you are in can make you a different person. Change is sometimes good, especially if you are changing for the better and with someone positive.

When Damion started his new school as a senior, he fit right in. He became very popular; he was no longer "a mama's boy" or teased about his clothes. With his job and the help of his grandparents, he had nice stylish clothes, several pairs of nice tennis shoes, even a few nice suits and dress shoes. The skinny girls with the pimples had all matured, they had nice physiques and were very flirtatious. He was very proud of his "glow up". Damion had grown to six feet and four inches tall; he had spent a lot of time in his grandparents' basement and at his old school's gym lifting weights and working out. He had let his hair grow out, so he now had long twists with blond tips which he often wore up in a ponytail. Since he played football and basketball at his old school, he planned to continue to play at this school as well. His hopes were that he could get a scholarship to help him with his college education, which had been preparing for since he lived with his grandparents.

Chapter 8 – Parent support is gold

Every game that Damion had, he would always look in the crowd for his mother, but she never showed up and that really hurt him. Although she wasn't there during most of his high school years, he thought that maybe since he was closer to home, that she would be there to try and make up for lost time, but she never showed up. Neisha showed up and he was grateful, but he wanted support from his parents. Their basketball team made it to the championship, and he was pumped the entire game. It was the last quarter with one minute and twenty-two seconds left in the game and the other team called a time out. Damion was in a huddle with his teammates going over their next play, when he glanced into the audience seeing a familiar face, he thought about it for a few seconds, but then the whistle blew for them to go back to the game. They won the championship sixty-seven to seventy-two, which Damion scored seventeen points and had three assists in that game. He was ecstatic about the win and ready to celebrate with his teammates. Damion was on his way to the locker room when he heard someone call his name. He looked over and it was the same familiar face that he had eye contact with during the time out. He threw his head back to say what's up but kept walking as he didn't know who this person was or what he wanted. He stopped and looked back at the strange man, and he froze thinking *"I know this is not who I think it is and then again, it could be a recruiter."* He heard his coach's voice but didn't hear what he was saying. The man walked towards Damion and when he got closer, Damion knew that this was not a recruiter, but it *was* his father.

"Come here, son" said Swav, with the biggest smile on his face. Damion ran to his father and hugged him, not wanting to let go. "Dad!" he yelled as he began to cry. His coach realized what was going on and signaled to his father to send him to the locker room once they were done. They talked for a few minutes and Damion told him that he needed to go shower and change. Swav promised that he would wait for him, and that they could go get a bite to eat and catch up on old times. This was the best day of Damion's life. His team had won the championship and his father had shown up to his game. He later found out that Swav had been to several of his games. Damion remembered seeing him, but he hadn't seen him since he was five, so he didn't recognize him with the full beard and braids. He would have never expected to see his father at any of his games, since his mother never attended any, and the fact that his father was currently living almost two hours away.

"Dad, if you've been coming to my games, why is this the first time that you reached out to me?"

"Well, at your football games, I was never able to get close enough to talk to you. I waited after several of the games that I came to, but security is really tight around here and usually you guys get on the bus right away. It was pretty much the same at the away basketball games. I called your name, you always looked my way and did the same thing you did today, threw your head up as to say what's up and went on your way. I said that you probably didn't recognize me, it's been a while, but I wasn't going to give up. What made you stop today?"

"I don't know. I had this weird feeling and when I looked into your eyes, I just knew it was you." Damion and his father ate dinner and talked until the restaurant closed. They exchanged cell phone numbers and made a promise to keep in touch regularly. Damion went back to his mother's house and went straight to his room. He had no intention of telling his mother that his father came to his game because he knew that she would have something negative to say about him and the whole situation. Damion didn't want her to try to treat him any differently to try to outdo his dad because she was good at acting in that way.

> *Parents, especially fathers, don't realize that the smallest thing such as showing up to your child's games can make a difference. Our children need our support and father's matter. Most children these days are being raised in a single parent household and some don't even know their father and that is a problem. Being active in your son's lives and being a positive role model will not only teach your son how to be a man, but it will also show them the importance of*

being in their child's life, when the time comes.

Since Damion was staying back with his mother, he didn't work that many hours anymore because his job was closer to his grandmother's home. Since he didn't have a car and was playing sports, he really didn't have the time or the transportation to get to work; therefore, he mostly worked weekends. His money was dwindling down, but his father would give him a few dollars here and there when he saw him, but he was trying to get back on his feet as well. A few of the people that Swav hung with before he was locked up tried to get him back into the streets, but he was not interested, he had already lost too many years of his life that he couldn't get back. Swav had received his GED and taken a few culinary classes while he was in prison and after several rejections, he was able to land a decent job at a five-star restaurant that paid a decent wage, the hours weren't too bad, and it kept food on his table and the electricity on. And most importantly, he was able to help his son financially when he needed to.

Damion didn't get the scholarship that he hoped for but had planned on using all the skills that he had learned before graduating from high school to start his own business. He had taken a few vocational classes so that he could start a trade, which had given him a jump start straight out of school to start fixing up houses. He had learned how to run electricity, hang drywall, paint, lay tile floors and other home improvement tasks. Damion never let a learning opportunity get past him, he was always eager to learn. He used these skills to start a small business with another classmate. It was hard for them to get business because the company was new and not yet reputable. They had been trying to get their business off the ground for months, but they weren't having the luck that they anticipated. His classmate decided to pull away from the business and left Damion to manage on his own. He dreamed that he would get his name out there and start making thousands of dollars so, he had quit his job at the fast-food restaurant. Most of the people in the neighborhood that gave him an opportunity didn't want to pay him for what he was worth, which would leave him only making a small profit. He did great work, but most folks didn't want to pay fair. He usually settled for the lower pay, just to get the opportunity to do the job with hopes that they would tell others and his business would grow by word of mouth. He would post his work on his social media sites, which did get the attention of others, but once he quoted a price for the material and labor, once again people didn't want to pay fairly. They figured since they were in the hood, they should pay hood prices. A few of the older couples outside of the neighborhood who lived closer to his grandparents gave him some odd jobs to do and his mother's landlord allowed him to paint and put new floors and ceiling fans in his mother's house which he was paid for. He liked the work and told him that he would keep him in mind for his other houses in the future, but those were the only jobs that he was paid his worth for. Damion would put in bids on jobs, and it seemed like the white boys always got the job, even if his price to do the work was less. He started applying for jobs with larger companies just to get his foot in the door, but he didn't "have enough experience" even with the portfolio that he had prepared showing photos of his work, he was still turned down. Damion started to feel worthless, and his confidence started plummeting. He felt deflated and wanted to give up. He called his dad to tell him how he was feeling as he always gave him encouraging words and this time, he told him that "sometimes you may get fifteen no's before you get a yes and that one yes will be more beneficial than all of those no's. He encouraged Damion to keep his head up and never give up."

A lot of times it seems like African Americans must work three times harder than others to get ahead and it can be frustrating. We must learn not to sell ourselves short, stay educated and never lose faith. It is also good to have a positive person to receive encouragement from and to help keep your spirits up.

Damion thought about what his father said and decided he wouldn't fall short and do what society expected him to do by going to the streets. He decided to go back to school to gain more skills and get a degree, in hopes to have the opportunity to get hired with a reputable company, get his

name out there and continue to work on
starting his own business. He found a
school and talked to the administration
office realizing that he would have to take
out loans to continue his education.
Knowing that his father had been gone so
long that he couldn't help, he went to his
mother to share his thoughts.

"Mom, I want to go back to school to get a
degree so that I can move us out this hood."
"Boy, this ain't no TV show. We ain't going
nowhere." Damion ignored her negativity.
"All I need is for you to fill out the parent
loan portion for my student loan."
"I ain't putting my name on nothing. You'll
start going and don't finish and don't pay
your bills, I ain't getting stuck with that
mess."
"Come on mom, you know that I'll finish.
You said that I wasn't going to graduate
from high school, and I did, with honors. I
want a better job. You know how long I've
been trying to get a good job, and everyone

keeps telling me that I don't have enough experience? I see all these white boys, some that I graduated with, working and none of them have experience or went to school. It's not fair, It's so hard out here for a black man. You want me to be hanging on the corner sell drugs like every other brother in this neighborhood? Look where we are. These young boys are dying every day over senseless stuff. Do you want to die in this hood? Better yet, do you want **me** to die in this hood or be caged up like my dad was?"

"What are you trying to say? You have a roof over your head, running water, lights, heat, and food. What else do you need?"

"A piece of mind. It is so discouraging every time I try to get a job or bid on a job I get rejected because "I'm a black man"." I hate walking through this hood scared that I might get jumped, robbed, or hit by a stray bullet." Damion began to get emotional.

"All I can tell you is to keep trying, you'll get something. And what do you mean caged up like your dad was? Is he out?" Damion gave her a disgusted look, turned around shaking his head and went to his room thinking, if I sell drugs, maybe I can pay my own way through school.

We need to do better as parents. If your child comes to you looking for guidance or even encouragement to help improve their lives, we need to try to be there or at least guide them in the right direction. Some children actually want a better life than they are being brought up in and will sometimes do whatever it takes to get what they want if we are not supportive.

Chapter 9-The Power

One evening Damion was scrolling on social media and saw a post stating that someone was looking for help with a job flipping a house. This was an opportunity that he'd been waiting for. He inboxed the person responding in detail about the skills he could offer and about some of the jobs that he had completed while adding a few photos. That weekend, he was invited to go to the worksite to meet the owner and the crew and to see if he was interested in the project. The house wasn't in the best neighborhood, and the crime rate in that area was growing, so Damion arrived at the house about forty-five minutes earlier to watch from a bus stop a little up the street to see what the vibe was, if they were bringing in materials to fix up the house, and how many people were doing the job. A tall slim guy arrived first in a gray pickup truck with the company name on the side.

Damion watched as another guy got out of the passenger seat to help carry in the 5-gallon buckets of paint, drop cloths, brushes, and rollers. Damion waited a few more minutes and walked down to the house and knocked on the door.

The tall slim guy opened the door and Damion introduced himself. They went over the details of the project; the pay, their expectations, deadlines, a few other details, and Damion signed the contract. Damion was tasked with painting six of the rooms that were going to be all white in color. He had no problem with that task because he enjoyed painting. As the day went by a few more guys started coming in and working in other areas of the house. Three weeks had passed, and Damion was given other tasks to perform and was even offering his opinion on how other tasks should be done. A few of the guys were impressed with his work as well as his enthusiasm. The inside of the house looked very nice. Damion got along well with most of the workers, but there was this one guy, who was in charge while the owner of the company was not on the site, who would periodically give directives that Damion knew were not proper. He would listen but then go back to what he knew was correct because he didn't believe in skipping corners. He wanted everything that he touched to be done correctly. They were now moving to the outside to put new siding on the house. They all began working and Damion started measuring and cutting the siding and had it hung on the front of the house and under the windows. The guy in charge came over to check on his progress. "Lil' dude, you cuttin' these pieces too long. You just wasting material. If we can take some of this back, we can get more money." Damion was shocked that first off, he smelt a strong scent of alcohol on the man's breath, and he couldn't believe that he was asking him to cut corners for a few extra dollars. He explained the proper way to complete the task from what he learned in school. "Yeah, I've heard that before too", explained the man in charge, "but if you cut each piece about an inch or so smaller, it will still fit. This is how we do all our jobs, and when we return the unused material and take the scraps to the scrap yard, we can usually get about two hundred dollars back. We usually split it." Damion listened to the guy, but finished what he was originally doing but changed as instructed once he got to the top part of the house. When he was done, he didn't like the way that it looked. He didn't care about the extra money, he was more concerned about the job looking good, but it didn't... it looked sloppy, and he didn't want to do any more until the head boss came back. He called him and explained what the worker on site had instructed him to do and he was basically told to listen to what he was told and that he would look at it when he got there. Damion continued to do what he was told, shaking his head as he looked at the rest of the house. He could tell that a lot of shortcuts had been taken. He left for the day feeling disgusted. He caught the bus to his girlfriend's house so that he could tell her about his new job and how he felt uncomfortable with what he was being told to do and how he wasn't pleased with how things were looking. He wanted to quit as he didn't want his name associated with the outside work, but he needed the money; therefore, he was planning on going back the next day.

The boss came to check out the progress on the project and he was impressed with the inside. He started on the outside and gave praise to whoever had completed the lower section of the front of the house, which was Damion. After he looked at how good his work looked and started comparing it to the other completed portions, he could tell the difference. He liked what Damion had done. Some of the guys praised Damion and a few others had an attitude, especially the guy who told him to change the way that he was working. Damion was happy at first, but as the days went by the guys that weren't happy because he was doing a good job started picking with him. They would hide the material that he needed to do certain jobs or take the screws out of the boxes for the lights to make him search for ones that fit from the bucket of screws that they kept in the truck. He started arriving at the site early, when the boss was there, and gathering all the material and checking everything before he left. Then they would send him to get them lunch so that he wasn't able to work and then tell the boss that he was leaving and staying gone for long periods of time. They would tell

Damion that they would finish caulking and the next day it wouldn't be done. They would also tell the boss that he wasn't completing his portion of the work. When Damion was questioned about it, he explained that they sent him to get lunch and said that they would complete it and they denied it. Damion was new and the boss didn't say that he believed them, but the condescending conversations gave him the impression that he did. Damion finished the job so that he could get paid, but when asked if he wanted to help with the next job, he turned down the opportunity. He enjoyed the work and needed the money, but he didn't have time for this immaturity and ghetto mess. He knew this was a total set up and his peace of mind was worth more to him.

> *Sometimes it will be your own kind that tries to ruin you, or don't have your best interest. People don't*

*realize the negative effects that they
can have on a person. Just because
you are young, do what you know is
right. Taking shortcuts and not being
honest can hurt you in the long run.
Although Damion was new and
young, he knew what he was doing,
but he let someone who didn't have
his best interest change his honest
way of thinking and allowed them to
make him walk away from something
that he truly enjoyed.*

Chapter 10- A1 from Day 1

Damion told his dad about the job that he completed and how they were conniving and told lies on him. Swav explained to him that every opportunity that comes his way doesn't mean that it was meant for him and that he should be thankful that he had the opportunity to have the experience. Swav had Damion explain to him what he learned from this experience and what his plans were if this were to happen again in the future. Damion was disappointed because that job was what he had been looking for and what he enjoyed. What his father said made sense, and he knew that going forward he was going to do what was right and would just suffer the consequences, if there were any. He also wouldn't let anyone make him feel like he wasn't doing a good job because he wasn't doing it the way that they wanted him to. If he was pleased and the person that he was working for was as well, then that is all that mattered.

Swav remembered hearing about one of his former associates, Marcus, who had his own house remolding business. He had put the word on the streets that he was trying to get in touch with him. He even looked him up on social media. Marcus also used to be a corner boy. Once Swav was busted and arrested, Marcus switched gears and turned his life around. He went back to school and received his GED, started a family, and eventually got married. Marcus knew that Swav had a son but hadn't seen him since Swav was sentenced. Swav finally messaged Marcus letting him know that he was home from prison and gave him some history on Damion and his skills. He let him know that he was looking for some honest work and wondered if he needed any assistance. Several weeks had passed, but

Swav was joyful when Marcus responded,
providing his phone number, and asking
Swav to call him. They talked and Marcus
was ecstatic to hear from Swav and decided
to meet with him at a local restaurant for
dinner. They ate a good seafood meal,
drank a few beers, and talked for hours
about the time that they missed. They used
to write to each other on a regular basis,
but once Marcus got married and had
children, they lost touch. Marcus went into
details about his remolding company
ensuring Swav that he was licensed,
bonded, and insured. He explained how he
was really getting overwhelmed with his
work and could use some real help. Swav
told him all about the skills that Damion had
and about the guys that he was working
with repairing the house and how they had
treated him badly. He also told him how he
was trying to get work but was continuously
turned down and how he was getting
discouraged.

Marcus didn't know Damion as an adult but was willing meet him to see what kind of man he had grown to be, only because he was his homeboy's child. He told Swav that he would love to meet his son and see what kind of skills he had and asked him to set up another dinner for the three of them to talk.

Swav decided not to call Damion that night, as he wanted to talk with him in person. When he got off work that next day, he called Damion, who was at home lying on the bed moping. He told him to get dressed and to meet him at the high school. "Why, what's going on?" Damion asked. "I just want to politic with you. Are you hungry?"
"I ate some Ramon noodles earlier, but I got room for some real food. You know all we eat is struggle food around this piece. They get all those food stamps, but never buy

any real food. I don't understand, but anyways." Swav chuckled.

"I'll meet you in about forty-five minutes."

"Alright."

"One." And they ended the call.

Swav refused to go anywhere near Mary, or her residence and Damion truly understood why. He wasn't ready to face her after she had done him so wrong, after all he had done for her. She left him for dead and he would never forget that. He also didn't appreciate how she treated his only son so badly and how she interfered with their relationship by not allowing them to keep in contact while he was locked up.

Damion got dressed and walked down to the school where his father was sitting in the car waiting. They went to a restaurant to get meatball subs, fries, and a drink. While they were eating, Swav told Damion about the conversation that he and Marcus had the day before. "Now, don't get your hopes all up because he just wants to meet you and see what you are working with." Swav knew that Marcus was going to give him the job, but he wanted him to present himself like he would for any other job that he was applying for. "Although this is my dude, treat it like you are going on a job interview. I saw that little portfolio you put together, bring that along and show him what you are working with. Damion smiled the biggest smile that he had smiled since he had the first job presented to him, showing his pretty teeth and deep dimples. Damion was hoping that this opportunity was actually the one that he had prayed for. He was extremely ecstatic when he found out what his father had set up for him. They shook hands using the fancy handshake that they made up and finished their meal.

Sometimes it's not about what you know, but who you know, that will

open the doors for you to certain
opportunities.

The following week Damion, Marcus
and Swav all met at a high scale restaurant.
Damion wore a nice pair of tan slacks, a
purple button-down shirt, and a pair of
black dress shoes. He also sprayed a little
of his favorite cologne, POLO Red. He had
gone to his barber the night before for a
fresh lineup. He felt good, and his
confidence was high. He talked to Marcus
as if he'd known him all his life and Marcus
was impressed with the conversation as
well as the photos of the work that Damion
had completed. He asked Damion what
happened with the last job that he had, and
he explained that he wasn't really into bad
mouthing anyone, but he completed the job
per his contract and that it just wasn't a
good fit for him. All Marcus could do was
respect his answer as Damion was more
mature than he thought. At the end of the

dinner, Marcus paid, which was a relief to
Damion, although he was prepared to pay
for his own meal. He had only ordered
what he could afford, but this allowed him
to hold on to a few extra dollars until he
had more income than what he was
receiving from the part-time job that he had
returned to. Marcus stood up and shook
Damion's hand stating that he looked
forward to working with him and asked
about his availability. Damion couldn't
believe this was happening right now. He
felt it in his soul that this was the
opportunity that he was waiting for and a
way to make decent money, legally and
legit. Damion was currently only working a
few days a week at the hamburger place,
which made him available for Marcus the
other days. Marcus started off by seeing
how responsible Damion was. Although
Swav was his friend and he ensured him
that he would give him a chance, he still

needed to see how serious Damion was about working and if this would be someone that he wanted to hire full time on his team. He gave Damion the address of the site where they were working and instructed him to meet him the following Monday at eight o'clock in the morning. Damion was scheduled to work that day at the hamburger place, and he tried to request the time off or switch schedules with someone, but he had no luck. He decided that he would go in late as he felt this opportunity outweighed his current job.

On Damion's first day meeting with Marcus at the job site, he was 20 minutes early. He didn't have a car and wouldn't dare bother his grandmother with the task of transporting him around, so he caught the bus and walked the extra distance to get to the work site. This required him to get up at Six o'clock that morning to get there on time and Marcus was impressed to pull up to the site to see Damion waiting for him to arrive. He took him inside the house to show him what still needed to be completed, which was a lot. He also went over in detail what he and his crew had been working on, which was a renovation of an older home. The house was huge, two stories, four bedrooms, three bathrooms and a finished basement. They had forty-five days to get the house ready to be put on the market and hopefully sold. Damion walked around looking and smiling at the opportunity. Marcus asked Damion what he thought needed to be done. Damion ran down all the ideas that were running through his head as he was doing the walk through and once again, Marcus was impressed and decided to give him more responsibilities than he had originally decided. He wanted to see if Damion's skills were as good as his thoughts. Marcus asked Damion what materials he thought would be needed for the job and for him to meet him back at the jobsite on Thursday morning. This time at nine o'clock, as Marcus didn't want to interfere with Damion's current work schedule, but he knew from their previous conversation that he was off on Thursdays. Damion arrived at the hamburger place almost two hours late, since he had to catch the bus and his manager told him that there was no sense in him clocking in and that he could just go back to wherever he was that made him late. Marcus had never called off nor had he been late, and they treated him as if this was a normal routine for him. He didn't complain nor did he put up a fuss as he knew deep down inside that God had a better plan for him. Marcus went to his grandmother's house to check on her and then to spend time with his girlfriend, since he was in the neighborhood. He didn't want to take the bus all the way back to his mother's house; therefore, he stayed with his grandmother that night. This allowed him to be closer to his job at the hamburger place that he was forcing himself to return to the next day.

Damion didn't like his job at the hamburger place, but sometimes you must crawl before you can walk and settle for something that may not make you happy because it's convenient. Be patient and you will get to what you are striving for.

Damion set his alarm to wake him up at six-thirty the next morning to give him plenty of time to get ready and allow him adequate time to catch the bus. His shift was scheduled for nine o'clock that morning. His grandmother was already awake and making him a good breakfast that consisted of turkey bacon, western eggs, cheese toast and a glass of orange juice. She was so proud of her grandson. After he ate, she let him drive his grandfather's car to work so that he wouldn't have to be on the bus. Damion loved his parents and was so glad that he had decided to move in with them when he was fifteen and a half. They had helped him in so many ways. The summer after he first moved in, they sent him to driver's school and helped him get his license. He was now prepared for this journey. He stayed with his grandmother for the remainder of the week as he missed spending time with her as well as his girlfriend. This also allowed him to be closer to both jobs.

Thursday finally arrived and Damion was excited about his new adventure with Marcus. Damion's grandmother had allowed him to drive his grandfather's car

for the remainder of the week since he had
to work both jobs. He arrived at the job site
ten minutes early and sat in the car to wait
for Marcus. Once he arrived with a truck
full of material, Damion started to get
nervous. He got out to help him unload the
truck, taking a mental note of everything
that he had purchased. He was also
introduced to the other guys and a middle-
aged woman who were already helping
with the job. "I am going to start you off
with something kind of simple and I can
start showing you a little bit each day," said
Marcus.

"Bet!" said Damion, "simple like what?" he
asked.

"You can go in there," Marcus said pointing
to one of the rooms that had trash on the
floor. "And sweep up all that trash."
Damion gave him a distraught look thinking
here we go again, and Marcus started
laughing. "I'm messing with you man... how
are your drywalling skills?" "Actually, they

are really good." Damion said with confidence.

"Good!" Marcus gave him the instructions for his assignment and asked him not to mud the drywall until he observed his work. He hadn't seen any of his work outside of the pictures that he showed him. Damion put his air pods in, turned on his play list, put his phone in his pocket and went to work. He worked six hours that day. He was happy and so was Marcus. Damion was offered the job as an intern for now, working twenty-five hours a week, paying him four hundred and twenty-five dollars a week. Marcus didn't want to give Damion too many hours, he wanted him to have the opportunity to see if this was really what he wanted to do. He also didn't want to interfere with his current occupation, and he wanted to see how dedicated Damion was. This was the most continuous money that Damion had ever made. He got into his grandfather's car with tear filled eyes of joy.

He sat there for a few moments while he thanked God for allowing him to go through the trials and tribulations that he experienced with the other company and allowing him to not give up on his dream. He thanked Him for keeping his head in the right place when his mom and her boyfriend tried to guide him in the wrong direction. He thanked Him for the opportunity to have his father back in his life and prayed that this work opportunity would be good for him and not toxic. He smiled as he put on his seat belt and headed back to his grandmother's home to tell her about his first day and how they brought him on as an intern with a decent pay. He first stopped at a drive-thru to get them both a chicken sandwich, fries, and a milkshake. They ate, watched a movie and he fell asleep on the living room floor. His grandmother covered him with a blanket and then went to bed.

The next morning, Damion woke up and got dressed to get ready to head to his mother's house. His grandmother was sitting at the kitchen table going through some papers. "Are you about to leave?" she asked.

"Yeah, I am going to go to my mom's house to try to get some stuff together before the week begins."

"Oh" his grandmother said looking confused.

"Is there something wrong, grandma?"

"Uh, no. I just thought that you would stay a little longer. I had somewhere I wanted you to go with me."

"I can. Do you want to go now?" His grandmother smiled. She stood up, grabbing some papers and kissed her grandson on the forehead.

"Let me grab my purse. You can drive, I just need to go to the plaza over the way to take care of something." They got into the car and headed to the plaza. When they

arrived, she had him park in the parking lot
of the license bureau. "Do you want me to
wait in the car?" Damion asked.
"No, you will need to come in for this, but I
need one dollar." Damion was confused,
but he reached into his back pocket, pulled
out his wallet and took out one dollar. He
handed it to his grandmother, and they got
out of the car. When they were inside the
title bureau, his grandmother registered his
grandfather's car over to him. She used the
dollar that he had given her in the car for
the purchase price of the car. Damion
shook his head as he smiled, kissing his
grandmother on her forehead "love you
grandma." His grandmother was always
looking out for him. He had no clue as to
what else she had in store for him. The next
stop was to get the legal forms to add
Damion as the beneficiary to her home.
She knew that she was getting older and
didn't have anyone else that she wanted to
leave her house to. Damion had grown up

to be a respectable and responsible young man, and she was proud of him. She knew that he would do the right thing as far as taking care of her home. She didn't feel comfortable leaving it to Mary. Although Mary was grown and her only child, she still had a lot of growing up to do. Grandma didn't want what she and her husband worked so hard for to get taken away. She knew that Mary wouldn't keep up on the taxes and insurance on the house but knew that Damion would.

Mary was trying to be more active in her son's life, but at this point he was an adult and basically taking care of himself. He had his grandmother and his father, the two people he felt were genuine and played a big part in his life. Although his father couldn't be there during all his childhood, when he needed him the most, he was there now and making up for the lost time.

www.ingramcontent.com/pod-product-compliance
Lightning Source LLC
Chambersburg PA
CBHW010450100726
47904CB00008B/2549